POND GOOSE

THIS BOOK BELONGS TO

..........Jack Welford..........

Happy Easter, 2005

For David

OXFORD
UNIVERSITY PRESS
Great Clarendon Street, Oxford QX2 6DP

Oxford University Press is a department of the University of Oxford.
It furthers the University's objective of excellence in research,
scholarship, and education by publishing worldwide in

Oxford New York

Auckland Bangkok Buenos Aires Cape Town Chennai
Dar es Salaam Delhi Hong Kong Istanbul Karachi Kolkata
Kuala Lumpur Madrid Melbourne Mexico City Mumbai Nairobi
São Paulo Shanghai Taipei Tokyo Toronto

Oxford is a registered trade mark of Oxford University Press
in the UK and in certain other countries

Text and Illustrations © Caroline Jayne Church 2004

The moral rights of the author/artist have been asserted

Database right Oxford University Press (maker)

First published 2004

British Library Cataloguing in Publication Data available

ISBN 0-19-279136-2 (hardback)
ISBN 0-19-272571-8 (paperback)

10 9 8 7 6 5 4 3

Originated by Dot Gradations Ltd, UK

Printed in China

JP

POND GOOSE

Caroline Jayne Church

OXFORD
UNIVERSITY PRESS

Down on the farm lived a gaggle of geese.
They were shiny and clean.
Even their beaks gleamed.

All the geese, that is, except one.

One little goose splashed alone in a muddy pond.

He wasn't shiny or clean.

And his beak certainly did not gleam.

The other geese laughed at him.
'Look at Pond Goose!' they honked.
'Mucky little Pond Goose!'

Most of the time all the geese led a very happy life. But when the full moon shone they would tremble with fear.

A full moon meant
only one thing...

...the fox would come!
And **Whoosh!**
Down the hill he'd
chase all the geese,
through the woods
and all around
the farm.

The fox chased all the geese, that is,
except one. He never chased Pond Goose.

One morning, after a very bad chase, the geese had just had enough. It was time to talk to Pond Goose.

'Why doesn't the fox ever chase you?' they demanded. 'Have you got a secret you're not telling us?'

'No,' said Pond Goose. 'It's because of my muddy feathers. They blend into the shadows so the fox can't see me. Not even by the light of a full moon.'

All the geese looked at each other...

...and ran to the nearest muddy pond!

Time went by and all the happy,
muddy geese pecked away
on the hillside.

All, that is, except one.

Pond Goose watched the sky — it was heavy
and grey. He shivered. It could mean only one thing.

He called to the others and tried to explain
but they wouldn't listen.

So he set off alone once more,
this time to find a clean, clear pond.

There he washed and scrubbed,

scrubbed and washed,

until all his feathers were clean and gleaming.

That night the moon rose,
full and round. And **whoosh!**
The fox chased all the geese once again.

All the geese, that is, except one.
The fox didn't see Pond Goose . . .

And he didn't see his
foot either. **Bam!**
With a **bump** and a **thump**
he fell into the snow and rolled down the hill.
The fox rolled faster and faster . . .

...further and further,
   far, far away out of sight.
      'He's gone!' cried the geese.
         'I don't think he'll be back, either,' smiled Pond Goose.

'Oh, thank you, Pond Goose!' said the geese.
And for the first time he felt one of the gaggle.